Gift-A-Book
2016-2017

This book was given to
Sunset Elementary
By
Mailie O'Connor

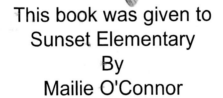

JIM BENTON

Franny K. Stein

MAD SCIENTIST COLLECTION

LUNCH WALKS AMONG US

ATTACK OF THE 50-Ft. CUPID

THE INVISIBLE FRAN

THE FRAN THAT TIME FORGOT

ALSO BY JIM BENTON

JIM BENTON

Franny K. Stein

MAD SCIENTIST COLLECTION

LUNCH WALKS AMONG US

ATTACK OF THE 50-Ft. CUPID

THE INVISIBLE FRAN

THE FRAN THAT TIME FORGOT

SIMON & SCHUSTER BOOKS FOR YOUNG READERS

NEW YORK LONDON TORONTO SYDNEY

SIMON & SCHUSTER BOOKS FOR YOUNG READERS
An imprint of Simon & Schuster Children's Publishing Division
1230 Avenue of the Americas, New York, NY 10020
Lunch Walks Among Us copyright © 2003 by Jim Benton
Attack of the 50-Ft. Cupid copyright © 2004 by Jim Benton
The Invisible Fran copyright © 2004 by Jim Benton
The Fran That Time Forgot copyright © 2005 by Jim Benton
All rights reserved, including the right of reproduction in whole or in part in any form.
SIMON & SCHUSTER BOOKS FOR YOUNG READERS
and related logo are registered trademarks of Simon & Schuster, Inc.
Also available in a Simon & Schuster Books for Young Readers hardcover edition and Aladdin Paperbacks edition.
Designed by Lucy Ruth Cummins and Dan Potash
The text of this book was set in Captain Kidd.
The illustrations for this book were rendered in pen, ink, and watercolor.
Manufactured in the United States of America
0610 FFG
First Aladdin Paperbacks edition April 2009
2 4 6 8 10 9 7 5 3
Library of Congress Control Numbers
Lunch Walks Among Us: 2003009362
Attack of the 50-Ft. Cupid: 2003018635
The Invisible Fran: 2004007425
The Fran That Time Forgot: 2004011638
ISBN: 978-1-4169-9392-6

Franny K. Stein

MAD SCIENTIST

LUNCH WALKS AMONG US

JIM BENTON

For Griffin,
Summer,
and Mary K

CONTENTS

CHAPTER ONE

FRANNY'S HOUSE

The Stein family lived in the pretty pink house with lovely purple shutters down at the end of Daffodil Street. Everything about the house was bright and cheery. Everything, that is, except the upstairs bedroom with the tiny round window.

That room belonged to Franny K. Stein, and she liked to keep it dark, and spooky, and creepy.

Every few days her mother would come in and redecorate Franny's bedroom with daisies, and lilacs, and pictures of lovely horses. It would always look so sweet and pretty.

But by the very next day Franny would somehow manage to make it look dark, and creepy, and spooky again. That was how she liked it—like a dungeon, complete with giant spiders and bats.

"Bats! Where does she get bats?" her mother would ask when she saw Franny's room. "Is there a bat store around here or something?"

Of course there wasn't a bat store around. The bats just kept showing up. The bats liked Franny's room, and Franny liked the bats.

"They're like rats with pterodactyl wings," she'd say. "What's not to like?"

CHAPTER TWO
FRANNY'S ROOM

ranny's bedroom was really something special. It had big steaming test tubes, strange bubbling beakers, and a whole bunch of crackling electrical gizmos that Franny had made all by herself.

Franny's room also had a giant tarantula cage, a snake house, and a tank where she raised a special breed of flying piranha. She couldn't imagine why anybody would want daisies and lilacs when they could have poison ivy and Venus flytraps.

"There's no comparison," she'd say, ducking one of her flying piranha.

Franny thought her room was so great, and so wonderful, and so perfect for her that she almost never wanted to leave it. But she had to, of course, for things like going outside, eating dinner, going to school, and using the bathroom.

Which is something Franny really liked to do.

Whoops. That didn't sound right. It was going to *school* that Franny really liked.

CHAPTER THREE

NEW AT SCHOOL

Franny and her family had just moved to the house at the end of Daffodil Street, and she was new at school. She liked her teacher, Miss Shelly. She thought she would like the other kids, too. But they really weren't very friendly toward Franny.

The other kids weren't mean; they just had never known anybody like Franny.

Nobody else had a jump rope like Franny's.

Franny's lunches didn't look like the other kids' lunches either.

And when they played hide-and-seek, no one could find her.

Franny could tell that the other kids were afraid of her, and that made her sad, because she really did want to make friends.

Her teacher, Miss Shelly, noticed what was happening. And one day she asked Franny to stay after class.

CHAPTER FOUR

A PROPOSAL

Miss Shelly was the nicest, smartest teacher Franny had ever had. Franny used to think that if only she dressed differently and wore her hair another way, she would be perfect.

"You're a wonderful student," Miss Shelly said.

"Thank you," Franny said. "I like school. Especially science. Especially the gooey parts of science."

"I like the gooey parts too," Miss Shelly said, and they both laughed.

"I'm a mad scientist, you know," Franny whispered.

"That must be very rewarding," Miss Shelly said, but she didn't really believe that Franny was a real-life mad scientist. Franny could tell.

"But I wonder if you might be a little lonely sometimes," Miss Shelly continued.

"I am lonely, sometimes," Franny admitted. "But I don't understand the other kids, and I don't know how to make friends with them."

"I think you can figure it out," said Miss Shelly. "You're smart."

Franny folded her arms. "I don't know, Miss Shelly ..."

"Think of it as an experiment," Miss Shelly said.

Franny's eyes lit up. A wide grin crawled across her face. An experiment was the one thing she just could not resist, and Miss Shelly knew it.

"The experiment"—Franny pointed into
the air the way mad scientists do when they
think about conducting an experiment—
"begins tomorrow."

CHAPTER FIVE

THE EXPERIMENT BEGINS

The next day Franny came to school prepared to start her experiment. Before class she observed some of the girls playing with dolls. Franny was delighted. She knew about dolls.

She loved dolls. In fact she loved them so much that she had even made some special modifications to the ones she had at home.

Chompolina

FASHION DOLL BY
F.K. STEIN

CHOMPOLINA'S
STEEL TEETH
CAN EASILY MUNCH
THE HEADS OFF OTHER DOLLS!

SUPER DANGEROUS!

Oozette

CUDDLY DOLL
BY F.K. STEIN

OOZETTE GUSHES
STICKY GUNK
WHENEVER YOU
HUG HER! ♥

She was just about to tell the girls how Chompolina could bite the heads off their dolls when she noticed something. Their dolls were all kind of . . . sweet, and pretty. They all had long hair and flowery dresses. Not a single one of them oozed uck. They didn't ooze anything.

Franny made a note to herself: *Pretty, non-head-biting dolls,* it said. *And less oozing.*

At lunchtime Franny sat down at a table with a bunch of kids. She was getting ready to take out her exquisitely delicious crab ravioli in pumpkin sauce when she made another observation.

Peanut butter and jelly sandwiches on her left, lunch-meat sandwiches on her right. As far as Franny's eyes could see was a carpet of soft, white, squishy sandwiches.

No casseroles, no stews, no shish kebabs; just sandwiches.

"Is this all they ever eat?" she whispered to herself. And she made another note: *Squashy sandwiches*, it said. Franny stuffed her lunch into the trash.

During recess the kids decided to play soft-ball. "I have the ball," one of them said.

"But we need a bat," another one said.

A bat! Franny thought. *Finally. Something I understand!* She reached into her backpack to get one.

Just then a little boy ran past her with a baseball bat. "Batter up!" he shouted.

"Hmmm," said Franny. "There's more than *one* kind of bat."

As her classmates started playing, she took out her notebook and made another note: *A bat can also be a big stick you use to hit things*, she wrote.

After school Franny picked up her backpack full of customized dolls, and spiders, and notes, and bats, and headed home to analyze the data she had gathered that day.

Chapter six

BACK AT THE LAB

Back in her room Franny looked over her notes. She made some calculations and puzzled over her findings.

"Nice kids," she said finally. "Kind of boring, but really nice."

That night Franny dreamed about how much fun it would have been to play dolls with those girls or to trade sandwiches at lunch. Even softball looked like fun, in spite of the fact that they used the kind of bat that didn't have cute, veiny wings.

CHAPTER SEVEN
MAKING MONSTERS

Early the next morning, as she was getting ready for school, Franny pulled down her copy of *A Treasury of Monster-Making Techniques* and turned to the chapter on transformations. In particular she studied the part that explained how to transform a little girl mad scientist into something else.

FRANNY'S BOOK ON MONSTER MAKING

Carefully cut on the dotted lines on
JUST THE NEXT TWO PAGES!

Flip the sections back and forth and see what
the recipe calls for to construct each
particular monster you create.

WARNING
We assume no responsibility if you actually
create a real monster and it destroys your
city and eats your stuff.

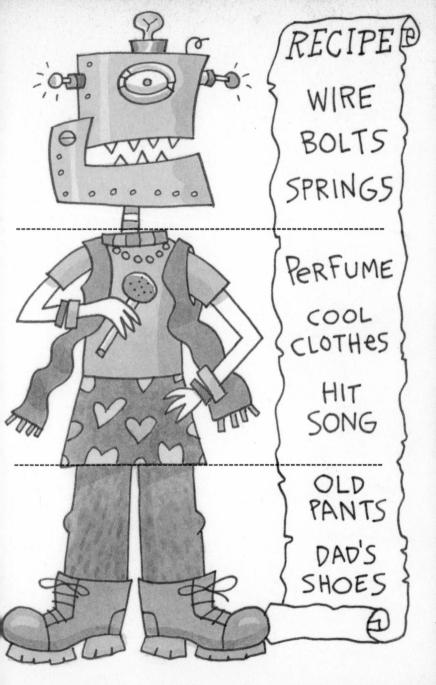

RECIPE

WIRE
BOLTS
SPRINGS

PERFUME
COOL
CLOTHES
HIT
SONG

OLD
PANTS
DAD'S
SHOES

RECIPE

SHAMPOO
BLUSH
LIPSTICK

ZOMBIE
BODY

STINKY
VEST

WORMS

BALLOONS
POPCORN
COTTON
CANDY

41

RECIPE

ZOMBIE
HEAD

LIGHTNING

ROACH
BUTTS

SPIDER
LEGS

DANCE
LESSONS

CHUNKY
HEELS

43

"I know just what to do," she said, and she began combining honey, vanilla jelly beans, and pink soda. She poured the formula into a tall, pretty glass decorated with a happy sheep holding a puppy wearing diapers.

"Ugh," she said. "How cute can you get?"

She put the mixture into one of her inventions, and programmed in her notes. The machine began to hum and shake, and buzz and bake, and then finally it binged, just like a microwave when your microwave popcorn is ready.

Franny gazed at the potion. She held her nose and drank it. She ran to the mirror and watched a strange transformation take place.

47

FRANNY TRANSFORMS

Carefully cut on the dotted lines on
JUST THE VERY NEXT PAGE!

Flip the sections and watch,
in horror, how Franny
transforms.

49

When Franny came downstairs to breakfast, her mom took one look at her and dropped her toast. Her dad choked on his coffee. Her brother's eyes almost popped out of his head.

"Franny," her Mother said, "you look so...nice."

Franny did look nice. Her hair was cute. Her dress was pretty. Her shoes were adorable. She didn't really look like Franny anymore, but she looked nice—kind of.

"Thanks, Mom," she said. "Here's a description of something I'd like prepared for lunch. It's strange, and horribly exotic, but I'd appreciate it if you could give it a try."

Her mom looked at the recipe that Franny had given her. "This says 'jelly and peanut butter between white bread slices,'" she said. "I'm pretty sure I can make this, Franny. I've been making it for years."

"Excellent," Franny said, and she rubbed her hands together in a mad-scientist way.

CHAPTER EIGHT

A TRANSFORMED FRANNY

Before school Franny met some of the girls from her class. Franny had a modified Chompolina with her.

Now Chompolina played happy music and squirted perfume and glitter and came with her own nail polish and a rainbow-colored unicorn with a long tail you could braid.

The other girls loved Chompolina and crowded around her.

Franny thought it was fun playing with the girls, but deep down she missed the old Chompolina.

At lunchtime Franny pulled out her PBJ sandwich. The peanut butter had been artfully smoothed, and the jelly had been applied equally from one corner to the other. The bread was so blazingly white that Franny needed sunglasses to look at it. Her mom had even trimmed the crusts, and the other kids, noticing this, smiled with approval.

Franny took a bite and found it to be totally, completely, and incredibly ... average, uninteresting, and no big deal. She had expected so much more.

But her experiment seemed to be working, so she finished the mushy sandwich.

At recess Franny suggested they play soft-ball. She consulted her notes quickly and added, "I think it best we use a ball instead of a skull, or giant squid eyeball, or something gruesome like that."

The other kids were a bit puzzled, but they agreed.

Franny had fun playing with them, but deep down she knew the game would have been much more fun with a skull or giant squid eyeball.

After school the kids all said good-bye and a few even asked her to come over to their houses and play. It was great to be asked, but Franny had to hurry straight home and analyze her day. She was happy. The other kids liked her, even if it was only a *transformed* her.

CHAPTER NINE

LUNCH DOESN'T AGREE WITH ME

The next day at school, while the kids were doing their math problems, Miss Shelly took Franny over to one side and talked to her.

"How's the experiment going?" she asked.

"It's great. I understand them, and I think we're becoming friends. They seem to like me better if I just go along with the things they like."

"Are you sure that's for the best?" Miss Shelly asked.

"Well, that's what the data seem to suggest," Franny said, and showed Miss Shelly some graphs to back it up.

"But I like the real you." Miss Shelly was about to continue, when a piercing scream tore through the room.

SQUID EYEBALL
AERODYNAMICS

"The trash can!" a little girl shrieked. "It's moving!"

Franny's mad scientist brain raced. That was the trash can in which she had dumped her crab ravioli in pumpkin sauce two days ago. But an old lunch, all by itself, was not enough to start a paranormal reaction.

"Who else put something in that can?"
Franny said.

"I spit out my gum in there," one girl said.

"I threw a pair of old gym shoes in there,"
another boy said.

"I saw the janitor dump some trash in
there," another girl said.

"Egad," said Franny. "That was close. Well,
as long as NOBODY put any unstable industrial
waste in there, we should be fine."

"Oh, yeah," said one little boy. "I forgot. I
put some unstable industrial waste in there."

"Gadzooks!" Franny shouted. "That is the exact formula for a Giant Monstrous Fiend."

The other kids looked at her. They looked scared, not just of the mention of a Giant Monstrous Fiend, although the prospect of a Giant Monstrous Fiend was no comfort. They were also afraid of Franny. They were looking at her the way they used to, before they had become her good friends.

"I mean," Franny stammered, "that's what I would think if I was a weird mad scientist-type little girl, which, of course, I'm not."

They all smiled at her again.

Just then the trash can erupted like a volcano. As the smoke settled, the kids saw, for the first time, the type of Giant Monstrous Fiend that a mad scientist-type girl would have predicted.

CHAPTER TEN
THAT'S NO JACK-O'-LANTERN

The Giant Monstrous Fiend stood there chewing gum and breathing angrily. Its head was a pumpkin, and its body looked like a crab's. It was wearing the old shoes, and it was just dripping with industrial waste.

Franny hoped it would just jump out the window and go away.

And, to her surprise, the Pumpkin-Crab Monster jumped out the window and went away.

Unfortunately it grabbed Miss Shelly before it left. With a crash and a scream, the Pumpkin-Crab Monster and her teacher were gone.

The kids just stood there. They didn't know how to help. A few tried crying. A few tried screaming. One tried wetting his pants, although later on he admitted he had no idea why he thought that might help.

Some of Franny's new friends hugged her and shrieked, but Franny didn't shriek.

Franny *thought*.

Out the window the Pumpkin-Crab Monster was climbing the flagpole with Miss Shelly.

There was no way that Miss Shelly was going to get away from that monster thing. It was holding her tight, and it was climbing higher and higher.

Franny looked at her friends. She really liked them, and she was happy they liked her. She had hoped they would always be her friends, but still she knew what she had to do. Franny reached into her backpack and pulled out a vial. It said ANTIDOTE on it.

"Uh, guys," she said gently. "If you all get your lunches, I think I know what we might be able to do."

The kids ignored her. They just ran around in little circles, getting more and more scared and confused.

"Guys, really. I think I know what we need." Franny spoke a little louder this time, but they still ignored her.

"We need a fireman," one girl said.

"We need a superhero," one boy said.

"We need dry pants," said you-know-who.

Franny stood up. Outside, lightning cracked.

"What we need," she said, "is a mad scientist. WHICH I AM." She uncorked the antidote and drank it.

She began to cough and sputter and spit. She fell on the ground and scrunched down in a little ball. She stood up and felt herself return to normal.

Franny, the little girl mad scientist, was back.

CHAPTER ELEVEN

IT'S MAD SCIENCE TIME

Franny looked at the kids. They looked even more afraid of her now than they ever had before. She thought about trying to be sweet or less scary, but that just wasn't going to get things done.

"Do as I command!" she said in her most scary mad scientist voice. "Go get your lunches!"

The kids stopped running in circles and ran to get their lunches. Mad scientists, even when they're only four feet tall, can be very persuasive.

"Put the bread in one pile and the lunch meat in another," she barked.

The kids did as they were told and quickly disassembled their sandwiches.

Franny was busy examining the bottom of the trash can. "I think there's just enough of this unstable industrial waste left to do the trick."

Franny worked fast. She told the kids exactly how to arrange the lunch meat and how to get the bread ready.

They were afraid, but they did what she said, and they did it quickly.

Being the only mad scientist around, she was the expert on unstable industrial waste, so she took care of that personally.

Then Franny pulled a needle and thread from her backpack.

"This will require absolute silence," she said, and the kids watched her begin stitching the lunch meat together.

Franny worked quickly as the kids watched in terror, occasionally handing her additional slices of salami or bologna when she so instructed.

They knew they were watching something not of this world, something that no human eyes had ever seen before, and in that moment the pants wetter decided to let loose one more time.

CHAPTER TWELVE
HAM, I AM

Finally Franny walked solemnly across the room and washed snips of ham and smears of mustard off her hands in the sink.

She sighed a deep, satisfied sigh and turned to gaze on her creation.

There, standing motionless in the middle of the classroom, was a giant monster thing made entirely of glistening, delicious bologna, salami, pickle loaf, and ham.

The time had come to provide this creature with the awesome power source it would need to come alive.

Franny grasped its salami nose and slid two batteries up its nostrils. "Awaken," she commanded. The creature's eyes slowly opened. It growled and looked at Franny. The kids clung to one another in fear.

"The flagpole," Franny ordered, and the creature began walking stiffly toward the wall. With a mighty punch it smashed its way through and headed outside.

"Bread!" Franny yelled, and the kids, following Franny's plan, began pushing the pile of bread over to the base of the flagpole.

The Lunch-Meat Creature grabbed the pole and shook it. Miss Shelly screamed, and the kids gasped.

"Shake harder!" Franny commanded.

The Lunch-Meat Creature shook and shook until finally the Pumpkin-Crab Monster dropped Miss Shelly.

CHAPTER THIRTEEN
THE FINAL INNING

Franny watched calmly as Miss Shelly fell toward the ground, screaming. Then, with the loudest *puff* sound anybody had ever heard, Miss Shelly fell right into the big, squishy pile of white bread, completely unharmed.

Franny turned to the Lunch-Meat Creature. "Now, my lunch-meat abomination, go get that pumpkin-headed creep."

The Lunch-Meat Creature grabbed the flagpole tightly and pulled until bologna-flavored sweat dripped off its forehead.

Finally, with a monstrous groan, the Lunch-Meat Creature ripped the flagpole right out of the ground, causing a very angry Pumpkin-Crab Monster to fall and hit the pavement with a ground-shaking crash.

The Pumpkin-Crab Monster got to its feet and growled. It began stomping toward the kids.

It was almost on top of them when Franny, the only kid that did not look worried, calmly whistled.

Suddenly a cloud of bats flew down from the sky and grabbed the Pumpkin-Crab Monster by the arms.

"Batter up," she said.

The bats flew as fast as they could with the Pumpkin-Crab Monster, and they headed right for the Lunch-Meat Creature, who had the flagpole up on its shoulder.

The bats dropped their burden just in time for the Lunch-Meat Creature to bring the pole around like a giant baseball bat and connect with the Pumpkin-Crab Monster as if it were a giant, stinky softball.

With a loud crack it went hurtling off into the sky, never to be seen, or heard from, again.

"Home run!" shouted Franny.

Then Franny turned around and saw the shocked and horrified kids huddled around an equally shocked and horrified Miss Shelly.

They looked more scared of her than ever.

Franny had the sad, sinking feeling that she had saved the day but had lost all of her friends.

CHAPTER FOURTEEN

EASY COME, EASY GO

I, uh, could probably take the Lunch-Meat Creature apart and make your sandwiches again," Franny offered weakly.

"And sorry about the flagpole, Miss Shelly," Franny said. "And about the wall my Lunch-Meat Creature smashed through.

"Sorry about your pants, kid," she said to the boy who had wet his pants and who was now getting pretty tired of people talking about it.

The kids all just stood there, trembling.
They didn't say a thing.

Franny turned away and walked home,
sadder and lonelier than ever before.

CHAPTER FIFTEEN

BACK TO THE GRIND

The next day Franny went to school as herself. There was no reason to pretend anymore. The kids were afraid of her and probably always would be. Worse yet, Miss Shelly was probably afraid of her now too.

Franny opened the door to her classroom slowly. Suddenly a giant cheer went up from the kids inside.

"Hooray for Franny!" they yelled. "Hooray, hooray, hooray!"

Franny looked around, stunned. The kids were all hugging her and thanking her for saving them.

"Thank you," Miss Shelly said and hugged her closest of all.

Franny was shocked. She fumbled over her words. "Uh, you're welcome."

"Your monster fixed the flagpole and the wall," Miss Shelly said. "And it did such a great job, the principal wants to hire it to work here."

The Lunch-Meat Monster waved and grinned proudly.

"You're the coolest, Franny!" the kids shouted.

"You're not scared of me?" Franny asked.

"Well, it would be hard not to be a little scared. I mean, you did make a monster out of cold cuts," one girl said. "But still, you're our friend. And that makes it all okay."

"Friend!" Franny said. "Yeah, I am your friend. Just the way I am, just the way you are. Friends!"

CHAPTER SIXTEEN
WEIRD, BUT I STILL LIKE THEM

They didn't always like the same things, but they were all still friends after that. The other girls decided that Chompolina and Oozette actually *were* pretty fun.

And Franny learned how to enjoy an occasional peanut butter and jelly sandwich.

And together they figured out a way to play softball with both kinds of bats.

It was an unusual friendship, but a great one. And considering how experiments often end up for mad scientists, Franny thought this one had gone pretty darn well.

Franny K. Stein

MAD SCIENTIST

ATTACK OF THE 50-FT. CUPID

Franny K. Stein
MAD SCIENTIST

ATTACK OF THE 50-FT. CUPID

JIM BENTON

For Summer and Griffin

and nieces and nephews Mark, Sean, Brad,
Laura, Tommy, Lauren, Jessi, Robert, Allyson,
Dan, Kristen, Rob, Scott, Evan, Laura, Elissa,
Eric, Brooke, Joe, Mike, Lisa, Ashley, Abbey,
and Tess

CONTENTS

Franny K. Stein
MAD SCIENTIST

ATTACK OF THE 50-FT. CUPID

CHAPTER ONE

FRANNY'S HOUSE

The Stein family lived in a pretty pink house with lovely purple shutters down at the end of Daffodil Street. Everything about the house was bright and cheery. Everything, that is, except the bedroom behind the tiny, round upstairs window.

This was Franny's bedroom, and she loved it more than anyplace else in the whole world, because this was where she came up with some of the most exciting new ideas in mad science.

But, as is often the case for mad scientists, it was impossible to get her friends and family to take her work seriously.

Like when Franny presented her recently perfected Personal Cow to her father.

"Hey, Dad. Have a look at this. I genetically engineered a real cow for the portability that today's baby-on-the-go demands. See? Fresh milk anywhere."

"That's nice, Franny," he said without even looking up from his newspaper.

Or when Franny tried to show off her just-debugged Biggerizer to her little brother, Freddy.

"One blast from this device can make things hundreds of times bigger," Franny declared proudly.

"Can you use it in reverse and make your mouth smaller?" Freddy asked.

Franny answered, "It doesn't have a reverse setting. It only makes things bigger, but that's not a bad idea...." Before she could finish, he leapt on his skateboard and, with one swift push, rocketed out of sight.

Or when Franny called Percy, one of her new friends from school, to announce her new Manifester. "You put a picture of something in front of it, flip the switch, and—*ZAP!*—it creates a real three-dimensional reproduction of it."

"Did you ever put ketchup on corn chips?" Percy asked witlessly.

5

Franny blinked. "Ketchup on corn chips? Did you hear a single word I said, Percy? The Manifester actually makes *real* things from pictures and pictures from real things. It's total madness."

"I like corn chips," he said, and Franny hung up the phone.

Franny's mom had been watching and she felt bad for Franny.

She might not have chosen to have a mad scientist for a daughter, but that's what Franny was.

And since that's what Franny was, her mom had spent a lot of time trying to learn about mad scientists.

One of the things she learned was this: Mad scientists need assistants to whom they can show their tiny cows, weird devices, and crazy gizmos, assistants who were always excited and who always listened.

CHAPTER TWO

FLEAS AND THANK YOU

One afternoon Franny's mom cautiously poked her head into Franny's room. When poking one's head into a mad scientist's lab, it's always best to do so cautiously.

"Franny, honey, I have somebody I want you to meet."

"I'm kind of busy here, Mom. I'm working on a machine that will make dirty socks smell worse."

"Why would you want that?" Franny's mom asked.

9

Franny paused, then said, "I guess you wouldn't, Mom. But that's how mad science works."

"Okay, but I just thought you might like to meet your new lab assistant."

"A lab assistant?" Franny said, totally forgetting about the sock experiment. More than anything, she had always wanted her very own lab assistant.

"Well," her mom said, "he's not a *pure* Lab. He's also part poodle, part Chihuahua, part beagle, part spaniel, part shepherd, and part some kind of weasly thing that's not even exactly a dog."

Franny stared blankly at the thing Mom had at the end of a leash.

"But he'll always be interested and excited about your projects, sweetheart, and you can teach him to be your assistant. His name's Igor."

Igor coughed and cocked his head. A few fleas hopped around in his fur. He could tell right away that he liked Franny, and he hoped she liked him in return.

"Oh. It's a dog," Franny said flatly, looking at Igor like he was half a glass of warm water. "I thought you meant..."

Franny was all ready to tell her mom to
take Igor away, but as she looked into her
mother's smiling face she could tell that her
mom had really and truly thought that Igor
was going to be a big hit.

She couldn't bring herself to let her mom
down.

"He's perfect, Mom," Franny lied. "Thanks."

"I just knew you'd love him!" Mom squealed, and handed Franny the leash.

Franny led Igor into her room.

"Sit here," she said. "If I need your assistance with anything, I'll let you know."

Igor sat and tried to smile the friendliest smile that a dog with a mouthful of pointy, craggy teeth could smile.

More than anything, Igor wanted to be a mad scientist's assistant. Especially if that mad scientist was Franny.

CHAPTER THREE

GOOD WHELP IS HARD TO FIND

Back to work," Franny said. Mad scientists are the hardest-working scientists of all. They do not allow interruptions like Igor to get in the way of progress.

Igor couldn't wait to help.

"Igor! Please don't touch the monsters."
Franny groaned when Igor tried to complete a
creature she had just designed.

"Igor! Hands off the devices." Franny
moaned when Igor tried to test her new X-ray
projector.

Igor helped Franny combine several extremely dangerous chemicals.

"Igor," she said. "Don't touch the test tubes. Please, just don't touch anything."

CHAPTER FOUR

LIFE'S RUFF

The next morning Igor watched quietly as Franny got ready for school. Before she left, she stopped to shake her finger at him.

"I think we've determined that you're a dog and not a lab assistant. So don't touch anything in this room except your dumb little rubber ball. Understand?"

Igor understood.

He concentrated on not touching anything except his dumb little rubber ball, because more than anything, he just really wanted to help.

CHAPTER FIVE

WHAT COULD BE VERSE?

Franny sat in class listening to her teacher, Miss Shelly.

"Now, remember that we'll be celebrating something special at the end of the week," Miss Shelly said. "You'll need to have valentines ready to share."

Franny raised her hand. "Miss Shelly, what are valentines?"

Miss Shelly never understood how Franny could know so much about weird things but so little about normal things.

Franny felt the same way about Miss Shelly.

The simple truth was that Franny, like most geniuses, studied the things she loved and didn't pay much attention to anything else, including holidays.

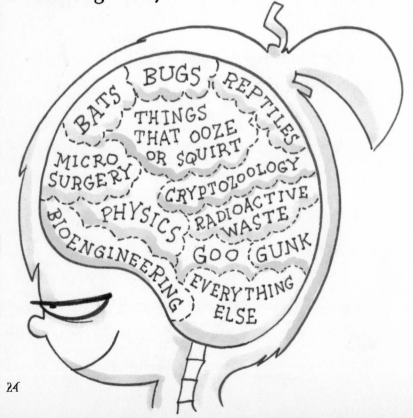

"A valentine is an expression of friendship or love," Miss Shelly began.

"Like for your mom?" Franny asked.

"Well, sure. You can send your mom a valentine. But valentines also celebrate love for those other than your parents."

"I'm not sure I understand," Franny said.

"Here's an example of something you might write on one," Miss Shelly continued. "'Roses are red. Violets are blue. Sugar is sweet, and so are you.'"

"And I write this on every valentine?" Franny asked.

"No, no," said Miss Shelly. "You try to personalize them. You know, express your feelings about the person."

"Okay. You're the boss," Franny said, although she had no idea what Miss Shelly was talking about.

CHAPTER SIX
FRANNY'S VALENTINE-POEM GENERATOR

Later Franny sat at her desk and worked on her assignment.

"I know just the thing to make this much simpler," she said triumphantly. "I'll create one valentine that will work for everyone. That will save a lot of time."

Igor watched quietly, although he really wanted to help.

The next day Franny showed her invention to Miss Shelly.

"It's called the Valentine-Poem Generator. You put the same thing on every valentine, and the recipient just chooses one section from each column. It's called a matrix. This way they can customize it for themselves. There are 625 different combinations."

FRANNY'S VALENTINE-POEM GENERATOR

Compose your very own valentine poem. Just take one section from each column and put them together in order.

Roses are red.	Violets are blue.	Sugar is sweet.	And so are you.
Pimples are pinkish.	I play the kazoo.	Turkeys are dumb.	Your family is too.
Boogers are green.	A clog is a shoe.	Bigfoot is hairy.	I believe this is true.
Weasels are brown.	You need a shampoo.	Oatmeal is lumpy	But much less than you.
Zombies are gray.	My toenails regrew.	Diapers are stinky.	This poem is through.

Miss Shelly smiled. She looked at Franny's card and then back at Franny.

"Franny, this is very clever, but maybe I didn't explain it very well. Perhaps adding some decorations or pictures might help."

"Oh, yeah!" Franny said. "Like pictures of the boogers and Bigfoot, right?"

"Well, I was thinking about a picture of something more traditional," Miss Shelly corrected. "Like Cupid."

"Cupid?" Franny asked. "What's that?"

"Well," Miss Shelly explained, "Cupid is this little naked guy with wings. He flies around shooting people with special arrows."

Franny was fascinated. "And people like him?"

"People love him." Miss Shelly laughed.
"And sometimes he has little hearts floating
around him."

Franny smiled. "Hmm, hearts. Well, I like
that part," she said.

"And he's always saying something mushy," Miss Shelly said.

"Mushy," Franny said as she took notes. "And this is all there is to this love stuff?" Franny asked.

Miss Shelly smiled. "Well, there are other things, like flowers and candy, I suppose, but Cupid is a good start, Franny."

CHAPTER SEVEN

DRAWING CONCLUSIONS

Back at home Franny looked over the notes she had made at school.

"Naked. Wings. Arrows," she mumbled. "And hearts."

She looked at her drawing.

"Oh, and he always says something mushy," she whispered. "Let's see—intestines are pretty mushy."

"I have the hang of this valentine thing," Franny said confidently, and she designed a few more, just for good measure.

Igor watched quietly, but he really, really, really wanted to help.

CHAPTER EIGHT

CUPID IS AS CUPID DOES

Franny couldn't wait to show her new valentines to her friends.

Miss Shelly followed the screams.

"See?" Franny said. "Cupid."

Miss Shelly gasped.

"I had a hard time choosing the mushy thing for him to say, but then I figured that nothing was mushier than guts."

Miss Shelly was speechless.

"Do you want to see the rest?" Franny asked.

Miss Shelly nodded.

FRANNY'S VALENTINES

VALENTINE, I HOPE YOU
ARE PUNCTURED TO A
SATISFACTORY DEGREE.

YOU WON'T BE
MY VALENTINE?

WELL, SUTURE SELF.

VALENTINE, YOU'RE
SUCH A TREASURE.

MAYBE YOU SHOULD
BE BURIED.

"Franny," Miss Shelly said finally, "you'd better have a look at this." And she handed Franny a real valentine.

CHAPTER NINE

PINK. CUTE. I'M GOING TO BE SICK.

Franny stared at the card. So *this* was what Miss Shelly was talking about. This was Cupid: all fat, and pink, and adorable.

"Ugh. Now, what is it that this guy does again?" Franny asked.

"He flies around and shoots his little arrows and makes people fall in love."

"Pretty horrible, huh?" Franny said.

Miss Shelly laughed.

Franny looked at her friends. She still didn't understand them, but she was crazy about them. So if a naked baby was what they wanted, that's what they were going to get.

"Okay, Miss Shelly. I understand now," she said, and Miss Shelly lent her the Cupid card to study.

CHAPTER TEN
WORKING LIKE A DOG

Late that night Franny sat at her desk staring at the Cupid card. She still had a lot of work to do if she was going to get cards for everyone done on time, but her heart just wasn't in it.

"I'm tired," she said, and tossed the card aside. "I'll finish the rest tomorrow."

Igor watched quietly, but he really, really, really, really, really, really wanted to help.

After Franny went to bed, Igor tried to sleep. But he was still upset about not being allowed to help. He walked around the room looking at Franny's marvelous experiments in progress and reminded himself not to touch them.

He couldn't think of anything to do, until he noticed, up on Franny's desk, his little rubber ball.

CHAPTER ELEVEN

THAT'S THE WAY THE BALL BOUNCES

Igor knew that he *was* allowed to touch the ball, so he carefully climbed up on the chair and reached for it. He took special care not to touch any of Franny's things.

Suddenly the wheels on the chair shifted, and Igor knocked the ball over the table edge.

The ball bounced twice, then hit the switch on Franny's Manifester.

The Manifester fired a beam directly at the Cupid card, which caused an itty-bitty, real-life Cupid to drop out the other side.

47

And—*zwing! zwizz! zwang!*—tiny arrows flew toward Igor as the tiny Cupid started shooting, which is exactly what Cupid is supposed to do.

Zwing! Zwizz! Zwang!

Igor dodged left and right. He made sure not to touch anything, just as Franny had told him.

Igor avoided jars he could've trapped Cupid in and a butterfly net he could've caught him with, because Franny had told him not to touch anything, and Igor was determined to do just as Franny had instructed.

49

Suddenly Igor heard a click and a zap, followed by a loud crunching crack. One of Cupid's arrows had bounced off a button on one of Franny's gizmos.

And that gizmo was the Biggerizer.

CHAPTER TWELVE

HEY MEISTER, WATCH THE KEISTER

A loud CRUNCH woke Franny and she looked up. Way up. Through the hole in the ceiling she saw the moon in the early morning sky. It looked pinker and squishier than it ever had before.

"Pinker? Squishier?"

Wait a second, Franny thought. *That's not the moon....*

That's the biggest baby butt the world has ever seen.

CHAPTER THIRTEEN

THE HOLIDAY IS UPON US

Franny jumped out of bed in a flash. She was standing right behind Igor as Cupid fluttered off like a big, adorable, incredibly dangerous blimp.

"Igor!" Franny said angrily. "Do you have any idea what you've done? I told you not to touch anything and you disobeyed me. Now you have released a monster that I don't know how to stop!"

Franny's eyes flashed with a terrible mad-
scientist madness that made Igor wilt.

"You're a *terrible* assistant!" Franny shouted
in a voice so angry that she didn't even sound like
herself. "And when I get back, you had better be
gone, you sad, ugly, good-for-nothing, little dog."

Franny snatched the Biggerizer and raced out the door. Igor sat there, brokenhearted, alone. He wondered where sad, ugly, good-for-nothing, little dogs were supposed to go.

Wherever that place is, Igor thought, *it sure isn't here.*

CHAPTER FOURTEEN
LOVE HURTS

All morning Franny followed Cupid's trail of destruction.

"He doesn't understand how big he is or how dangerous these huge arrows are!" Franny said. "He has to be stopped before he

skewers somebody!" Cupid, in the distance, was happily firing his arrows in all directions.

And heading right toward him was a school bus loaded with kids.

"Oh, no!" Franny yelled. "Cupid is going to love them to pieces."

CHAPTER FIFTEEN

LOVE IS A BATTLEFIELD

Franny arrived on the scene just as the bus driver saw the massive Angel of Love.

Immediately the driver hit the brakes. She tried to go in reverse. But the bus stalled instead.

Cupid noticed the stopped bus and the little kids inside, and he was sure they all wanted to be in love.

"Think! Think! Think!" Franny said as Cupid nocked an arrow on his bowstring.

The bus driver screamed.

The kids screamed.

Franny wished she had put a reverse button on the Biggerizer. Suddenly she thought of her brother. "Freddy!" she said, and she turned the Biggerizer on herself.

CHAPTER SIXTEEN

THE WHEELS ON THE BUS GO ROUND AND ROUND

C upid aimed, and—*twang!*—he released a giant arrow, sending it rocketing toward the bus just as Franny came hurtling through the air.

She slammed her right foot on top of the bus and dug her left foot into the dirt as she had seen her brother do countless times.

With a mighty push, Franny was off.

SMASH!

Franny weaved her way through the
streets, riding the bus like the biggest skateboard in the world.

Cupid flew after her in hot pursuit, firing
arrow after arrow, which Franny ducked and
dodged as she tried desperately not to wipe out.

I have to get back to my lab, she thought,
and she headed toward Daffodil Street.

CHAPTER SEVENTEEN

MOM ALWAYS SAYS TO WEAR YOUR HELMET

(WHEN YOU BECOME GIGANTIC AND SKATEBOARD ON A SCHOOL BUS)

Franny carved her way around a tight turn and hurtled toward home.

"This skateboarding is kind of fun," she said. "It's not nearly as hard as Freddy says it ..."

Franny bounced a wheel off the curb, breaking an axle and sending Franny flying.

"... iiiiiiiiiiiiiis!" she yelled as she tumbled through the air and landed on her front lawn with a very painful crash.

Cupid landed at the end of Daffodil Street and stomped toward the stopped bus. He had an arrow all ready to go.

This looked like the end.

Franny's head was spinning. She dragged herself in front of the bus and glowered defiantly.

Cupid pulled back on the arrow and again took aim . . .

. . . just as a mouthful of craggy, pointy teeth sank into his giant, squishy butt.

Cupid howled and jumped, and the arrow intended for Franny missed her by an inch.

As Cupid spun around, Franny saw Igor dangling from Cupid's sore pink rump.

Igor had saved her. He had saved the kids on the bus.

Cupid snatched Igor off his butt and threw him to the ground.

He was about to return his attention to Franny when he got a good look at Igor.

Igor was ugly. He was small and pitiful. But more than anything, Cupid could sense that Igor was heartbroken.

And broken hearts were something of great interest to Cupid.

"Good. Cupid's distracted." Franny groaned. "Now we can get out of here!" She started to limp away, slowly dragging the bus with her.

Cupid held Igor down with his big, fat, pink foot and stared at him. *This,* thought Cupid, *is the brokenest broken heart I have ever seen.*

This called for an extra-big arrow. Cupid reached for the biggest one he had.

CHAPTER EIGHTEEN

NO P.E. NOT TACOS.

Franny hadn't taken more than three feeble steps before she stopped. She remembered when Igor helped with the monster. *That actually was pretty funny*, she thought.

She remembered when he helped with her X-ray projector. *Also pretty funny.*

She remembered how he had risked his life to save her.

She let go of the bus. She was overwhelmed by a strange and powerful electrical charge crackling through her body.

A side effect of the Biggerizer? An injury to her nervous system sustained in the bus wipeout? Yesterday's cafeteria tacos not sitting so well?

Franny felt strangely empowered. She felt strong, and focused.

This wasn't high voltage. This wasn't a chemical reaction. This wasn't a supernatural phenomenon.

She looked at Igor.

"Egads," Franny whispered, and her heart melted.

CHAPTER NINETEEN

IT'S MAD SCIENCE TIME

"Must save Igor" was all Franny could say. But how? Franny's massive brain ran calculations and scenarios at a blurring speed.

Franny knew she could never take Cupid in a fight. He had that bow and arrow. And besides, it wouldn't be right to clobber a baby, even a fifty-foot one. A baby's a baby, right?

As Cupid put the arrow in the bow, Igor looked over at Franny.

"A baby's a baby!" Franny exclaimed. "He might be a gigantic, destructive, arrow-slinging Cupid, but he's still a baby!"

Franny pulled the roof off her house and tore through her beloved laboratory. "Where are you? Where are you?!" she yelled.

Finally she stopped.

"There you are!" she yelled, and fired the Biggerizer.

CHAPTER TWENTY

UDDER MADNESS

Back at the street Igor closed his eyes as hard as he could and waited for the twang of Cupid's arrow.

But he didn't hear a twang.

He heard a splash. Or was it splosh? It was that sort of squirty sound you hear when you turn the garden hose on full blast. Then he heard slurpy sounds and a moo.

He opened his eyes. Cupid was slobbering up
a long stream of some liquid.

And at the other end of the long stream was Franny.

She had used the Biggerizer on the Personal Cow and was squirting an irresistible gush of fresh milk. Cupid had dropped his bow and arrow and was following it like the big, chubby baby he was.

Franny maneuvered him to a spot where she could get a clean shot at him.

And while Cupid busied himself with the cow, Franny activated the Manifester in reverse. With one blast, she returned him to his proper form as the Cupid in a valentine card.

CHAPTER TWENTY-ONE

LGMS SEEKS ULD

(LITTLE GIRL MAD SCIENTIST SEEKS UGLY LITTLE DOG)

86

Franny stood in her yard. Cupid was no longer a threat and the kids were safe, but strewn on the lawn around her was the smoldering wreckage of her lab.

She should have been the saddest little mad scientist ever.

But she wasn't. She was happy. In fact, she was very happy.

Igor was okay, and as smart as Franny was, she would never ever be able to explain why, at that moment, that was the most important thing.

She stooped down and picked him up. He looked frightened and sad.

"Um, thanks for saving my life," she mumbled.

Igor trembled. He looked as though he would cry.

"You know," she said, "we mad scientists are sort of excitable. And, uh, sometimes we say things that we don't really mean."

Igor blinked. His eyes widened a bit.

"And really, this is all mostly my fault. I'm the one that made the Manifester and the Biggerizer in the first place."

Igor smiled a little.

"I guess what I'm trying to say is that I'm going to need an assistant to help me get back to normal size and also help put this lab back together.

"And, uh, I was thinking that I'd like you to be my assistant, if you want to. I'd really like it."

Franny felt that strange rush of electricity surge through her again. There was something about revealing how she felt that was almost as powerful as feeling it.

And, incredibly, it seemed to have an effect on Igor.

He sat up straighter. He somehow looked less ugly. His breath got better, and as he wagged his tail happily, dozens of fleas and ticks jumped off his back. They must have realized that Igor was no longer the type of dog that they could infest.

"You're going to be the best lab assistant in the world," Franny said.

Igor jumped from her hand and immediately started to help clean up the yard.

He knocked a flask into a beaker, which blew up, leaving a twelve-foot-wide crater in the yard.

"Okay," Franny said. "Maybe not the best.

"But you'll be MY lab assistant."

CHAPTER TWENTY-TWO
IT MUTTS BE LOVE

Franny and Igor worked together as if they had known each other forever.

They fixed the bus and got the kids off to school.

They built a device to shrink Franny back to normal size.

Along the way they learned that Igor could help a lot by holding things that Franny's giant hands would have probably broken.

And then they made all the Valentine's Day cards that Franny needed to give to Miss Shelly and her classmates.

"This thing is just too dangerous," Franny said, and together they destroyed the Biggerizer.

But not before they used it just one more time.

CHAPTER TWENTY—THREE

AND THAT'S THAT

Miss Shelly and the kids looked out the window. It looked like a giant brown mountain had suddenly appeared in front of the school.

"Happy Valentine's Day," Franny said as she walked in. She handed her cards to Miss Shelly and the kids.

"Franny!" Miss Shelly said. "Are you responsible for that, that *thing* out there?"

"I am," Franny said. "Happy Valentine's Day. It's for you."

"For me?" Miss Shelly said. "Really, Franny, I don't know what that thing is, but I'm quite sure I don't want it."

"Suit yourself," Franny said smiling. "But it's not a 'thing.'

"It's a chocolate-covered cherry."

Miss Shelly gasped.

"You said something about candy."

Miss Shelly and the kids went outside for a closer look, and Miss Shelly let them dig in.

"It looks like you were hit with one of Cupid's arrows," Miss Shelly said with a happy wink as she enjoyed a taste of the candy.

"I thought so too," Franny said seriously, "but after a complete examination, I found that I wasn't even nicked.

"No, Miss Shelly, there's something strange at work here, a phenomenon I just can't explain. It could take me months to unravel this."

"Months," Miss Shelly said, and she watched as Franny, Igor, and the kids slurped up the giant chocolate-covered cherry.

She opened the envelope that Franny had given her and looked at the card inside.

Miss Shelly—
He's the scariest thing in the world, but I know you like him, so, here's your cupid—
Love
Franny

And Miss Shelly felt that same strange surge of power that Franny had felt crackle through her from head to toe.

"Happy Valentine's Day, Franny," she whispered.

Franny K. Stein

MAD SCIENTIST

THE INVISIBLE FRAN

Franny K. Stein

MAD SCIENTIST

THE INVISIBLE FRAN

JIM BENTON

For
Kevin Lewis
and
Julie Kane-Ritsch

CONTENTS

Franny K. Stein
MAD SCIENTIST

THE INVISIBLE FRAN

CHAPTER ONE

FRANNY'S HOUSE

The Stein family lived in the pretty pink house with lovely purple shutters down at the end of Daffodil Street. Everything about the house was bright and cheery. Everything, that is, except the upstairs bedroom with the tiny round window.

The window looked in on a bedroom, yes, but it was also a window into a laboratory: Franny's laboratory. And Franny's laboratory was spectacular.

She had all of the things that you would
expect any mad scientist to have. She had an
electron microscope. She had a nuclear-powered
brain amplifier. She had a giant, flesh-eating
koala.

And she also had a few extras, a few special things that made Franny feel that her lab was just a little bit better than average.

4

Franny doubted that any other mad scientist had a spider enlarger or a disease simulator.

"I'll bet no more than half of them have an eyeball-removing machine," she said, thinking how fortunate she was that she could pull her own eye out.

But even if they didn't have eyeball-
removing machines or brain amplifiers or
spider enlargers, Franny suspected that her
friends—if given the chance—would love
nothing more than to set up labs of their own
and devote themselves to the pursuit of mad
science.

It was for this very reason that her teacher's next assignment inspired Franny to help her classmates see the light.

CHAPTER TWO

HOBBY DAY

Miss Shelly stood in front of the class. "We're going to talk about hobbies. Tomorrow I'd like each of you to bring in something that represents your hobby or interest."

Surely, thought Franny, *many of them don't even have hobbies or interests, and even if they do, they're probably the kinds of dull hobbies that hardly ever explode or eat the neighbor's car.*

9

Franny raised her hand. "Miss Shelly, if somebody has a hobby that doesn't involve massive amounts of electricity or sewing wings onto things that weren't born with wings, will they still be allowed to participate?"

Miss Shelly was accustomed to this sort of question from Franny.

"Yes, Franny. Everybody will get to talk about their hobbies," Miss Shelly said.

Miss Shelly was always fair, but it seemed like a waste of time to Franny, who was absolutely certain that after a little exposure to mad science, the kids would drop their other interests like hot potatoes—hot, radioactive, poisonous potatoes.

CHAPTER THREE

BACK AT THE LAB

Back at the lab Franny thought about what her presentation would be. Fortunately Franny had an assistant to help her with things like this.

Igor was Franny's dog and lab assistant. (He wasn't a *pure* Lab. He was also part poodle, part Chihuahua, part beagle, part spaniel, part shepherd, and part some kind of weasly thing that wasn't even exactly a dog.)

Franny had told Igor about Miss Shelly's assignment, and he was doing his best to make suggestions.

He reminded her of the time she had brought a garden gnome to life and they'd had to stay locked in the bathroom until the police came. Igor thought the kids would like that.

"I don't want to take in a garden gnome," she said.

He reminded her of the time she had increased the vacuum cleaner's power and had sucked her little brother inside out.

"Mom made me promise never to do that again," she said.

17

He reminded her of the time she had engineered a cannibalistic hot dog that actually ate itself.

"That *was* pretty good," Franny said. "But there's a kid in my class that always smells like hot dogs, and I don't want that thing going after him. Besides, it needs to be something that everybody can relate to."

Franny walked over and looked at the dozens of devices she had recently invented. "Like this, Igor." She picked up her toenail fungus translator. "You know, deep down inside, all kids want to communicate with toenail fungus, but they've never been able to.

"Well, with this device, they finally can."
She put it in her backpack. "All the kids will
love talking to fungus. I mean, c'mon, deep
down inside, we're all mad scientists, right?"

CHAPTER FOUR

OH NO, WE'RE NOT

Miss Shelly looked around the room. Everybody was ready to talk about his or her hobbies. She pointed at Erin.

"Erin, would you like to go first?"

Erin jumped to her feet and started a tape player. As the music began, she performed a classic foot-stomping Irish dance.

The students clapped.

Franny raised her hand.

"So, Erin, about these shoes of yours. Have you ever considered splicing in a sample of mutant kangaroo DNA? It might make you bounce around in an even more uncontrolled manner."

Erin looked at Franny for a moment. "My dancing is just fine, thank you," she said, and took her seat.

Next Miss Shelly invited Lawrence to the front of the class. He pulled an accordion from a big black case and played for a minute or two before Franny raised her hand.

"Ah. Now this is *much* better. I'm certain that you could operate the keys in different ways to increase or decrease the amount of pain we're experiencing around our ear regions. My question for you is this: Have you ever thought of making a larger version that you could attach to a satellite and use to broadcast this effect over a larger area?"

Lawrence put the instrument back in the case. "It's just an accordion, Franny," he said. "I've been playing it since I was a little kid."

Next up was Phil. Miss Shelly held a large book open for him while he pointed out the various prize stamps in his collection.

"This stamp is from England," he said. "And this one is from Japan."

Franny raised her hand. "I don't suppose you've considered altering these stamps so that they explode when people lick them, have you?"

Phil shook his head. "No."

"Or doing something like transforming the postal carrier into a—oh, I don't know—a nine-foot-tall scorpion man who spews acid from his stinger and can fly, for instance?"

Miss Shelly closed the book. "Franny, Phil prefers regular, nonexploding, nontransforming postage stamps."

"Hold on," Franny said. "Just hold on one second." She walked to the front of the class. "Do you mean to tell me that *none* of you is the least bit interested in being a mad scientist?"

CHAPTER FIVE

FRANNY TOSSES HER COOKIES

I gor sat patiently and listened to Franny.

"Not *one*," she said, dropping the toenail fungus translator on the floor. "In my whole class not one other kid has even thought about conducting an experiment! Dancing, yes! Collecting, yes! Athletics, yes! But mad science, NO!"

Franny continued her rant as she checked the progress of her various experiments. "One kid had a terrarium with a chameleon, but—get this—he doesn't do any experiments with it!"

Igor wasn't crazy about chameleons since the first time Franny's giant chameleon had tried to swallow him. But he shook his head and tried to appear as though he agreed with Franny.

"I asked Miss Shelly if I could put off doing my presentation until tomorrow. After Billy shared his hobby, which is making pretty, pretty cookies, my heart just wasn't in it. Pretty, pretty cookies. I mean, seriously, Igor, that has to be the dumbest hobby of all. Imagine doing all that measuring and mixing and waiting, just for pretty, pretty cookies. Look—he even brought some in for everyone."

Franny tossed her pretty, pretty cookies in the air and shot a sizzling death ray through them.

"These kids are so misguided, Igor. They don't know what they're missing. Their interests are absolutely useless. Maybe nobody has ever really showed them why mad science is really the *only* hobby on earth."

Franny stopped and grinned broadly. "That's it, Igor. It's up to *me* to show them where they went wrong. I can show them what they should be interested in. And I can see it's going to take more than a toenail fungus translator."

CHAPTER SIX

YOU MUST BE NUTS.
AND BOLTS.

Franny consulted a book from her library called *Mechanical Fiends and Hazardous Robots for Children.* Ultimately Franny created things the way she liked them, but a quick glance at some plans always got things rolling.

She worked most of the night, and with Igor's help she had a creation that she was certain would bring the kids around to her way of thinking.

CHAPTER SEVEN

WIRE YOU LOOKING AT MY ROBOT THAT WAY?

Franny sat at her desk, grinning. She couldn't wait to give her presentation.

"Franny," Miss Shelly said, "would you please come up here and show the class what you've brought in?"

Franny walked confidently to the front of the class. She knew that the kids would take one look at the robot and abandon their ridiculous hobbies.

She removed the sheet that had been draped over her creation. The kids gasped.

It was a robot. A few lights pulsed slowly on its chest, and they could hear a soft hum coming from inside it. Its tiny square eyes seemed to blink.

"Why does it have two heads?" one boy asked.

"Two heads are better than one," Franny said. "When it's complete, those two heads will make it *twice* as smart as the next smartest robot. Twice as useful, twice as complicated." Franny held up the robot's blueprints for the kids to see.

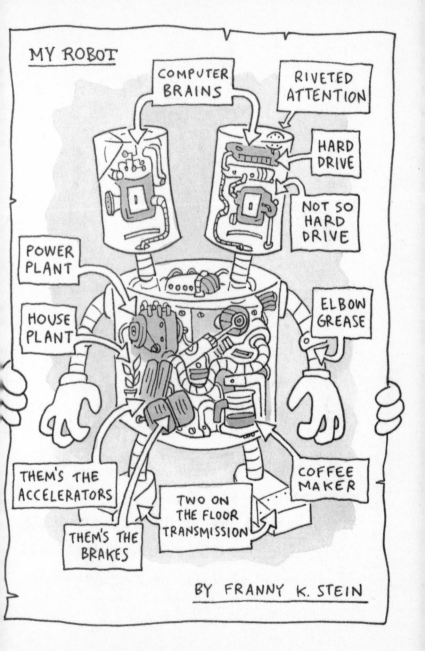

Miss Shelly said, "Franny, did you say that it wasn't complete yet?"

"That's right, Miss Shelly. It's *not* complete. I'm going to need other mad scientists to help me, other mad scientists *from the class*, perhaps. Are there any volunteers?"

Billy raised his hand.

Franny was smug. *The first of many volunteers,* she thought. "Yes," she said. "You'd like to help?"

"I would," Billy said. "After you finish it, I mean. Then I can teach it to bake pretty, pretty cookies."

CHAPTER EIGHT

IN THE GIZZARD OF THE LIZARD

Igor just hated to see Franny depressed. He did his best to cheer her up. He juggled spiders. He dressed up like her mom. He even thought about letting the giant chameleon swallow him a little bit, since that always made Franny laugh.

All Franny could talk about was her friends at school. "No volunteers, Igor. They all want to stick with their pointless little hobbies. They don't get it. They don't get it at all.

"They don't understand the thrill of an idea popping into your head out of nowhere, and then diving right in and making your idea just happen.

"If only they could experience that," Franny said.

Just then the giant chameleon appeared, as if out of nowhere, grabbed Igor, and swallowed him.

Even though she was depressed, Franny laughed a little and shook the chameleon until Igor fell out of its mouth. It's hard not to laugh when a reptile eats your best friend.

"You have to be more careful, Igor," Franny said.

Igor hid behind Franny.

"You know the giant chameleon can camouflage himself. It's practically like he's invisible."

Franny's eyes narrowed and a familiar grin stretched across her big, round face. "Invisible," said Franny, and she nodded slowly. "That's it. *Invisible.*"

CHAPTER NINE

LET ME MAKE MYSELF CLEAR

The next morning Franny combined cellophane molecules with chameleon DNA and some disappearing ink. She ran the formula through an Antiscope, which is like a microscope, but it's designed to make things harder to see. She poured the formula into a very, very clean glass.

She gulped it down and ran to the mirror to see if it worked.

She liked what she saw. Or, rather, she liked
what she didn't see, which was herself.

The formula had worked. She was invisible,
and it was time for school.

CHAPTER TEN

CHILDREN SHOULD BE HEARD AND NOT SEEN

Invisible at school. The temptations are hard to resist, especially for one with a mind as inquisitive as Franny's.

She had a quick peek in the school's cafeteria kitchen.

She zipped in and had a look in the principal's office.

She stopped in briefly to find out exactly what the teachers were doing in the teachers' lounge.

She found all of the locations fascinating,
but she had to get on to the next phase in her
plan: to get the kids to devote themselves to
mad science in a way that Franny knew she
should force them to want to.

Franny strolled into her class completely unseen. She walked up to Erin—who was reading—and whispered in her ear: "I think I'd like to have a look at Franny's robot again."

Erin set down her book and looked around, confused. "I-I guess I'd like to have a look at Franny's robot," she said, believing that she had thought what Franny had whispered. She walked over to the mechanical creature and began looking it over.

Next Franny did the same thing to Lawrence and Phil, and they, also believing the thoughts were their own, walked over and joined Erin.

Franny whispered to Phil, "It would be great if this robot had a huge, crushing hand, don't you think?" And Phil repeated exactly what Franny had said. Franny moved Erin's and Lawrence's heads to make it look like they were nodding yes.

All afternoon Franny kept giving them one idea after another. She also checked and double-checked that the adjustments they were making were correct. Erin, Lawrence, and Phil got more and more excited as they worked on the robot, believing that they were the ones responsible.

By the end of the day Franny was exhausted but happy. She had made a lot of progress on the robot, and her friends thought that they had contributed.

Back at home Franny took the invisibility antidote and told Igor all about the experiment. "It was a little bit funny, Igor. They really thought they were working on the robot. Of course they're not qualified to do anything that complicated yet," she said. "I'm not sure that Phil could even put batteries in a flashlight.

"But they had fun, and it boosted their confidence, and maybe now they'll stop wasting time on those ridiculous diversions."

Franny climbed into bed and drifted off to dream her mad science dreams, unaware that back at school something quite mad, but quite unscientific, was about to happen.

CHAPTER ELEVEN
SNEAKING OUT TO JOIN THE CIRCUITS

Erin, Lawrence, and Phil crept quietly into the school. They were wearing outfits unlike any they had worn before. They were dressed like mad scientists.

They had tools and notes and devices that
no real scientist would use to finish a partially
built robot.

And yet that is exactly what they intended
to do.

They surrounded the robot and waited for one of those brilliant "thoughts" to pop into their heads. But Franny wasn't there with her invisible whispers, so they just stood there, looking at each other.

After a while Phil became impatient and decided to pretend to have a brilliant thought. "It should be able to squirt ketchup from its nozzle right here," he said. The other two nodded.

"It needs to be able to extend this, like so," Erin said, also faking an idea.

"And I have a few changes I think we should make to its brain," said Lawrence, who sometimes had trouble changing his pants, much less a robot's brain.

"We are totally mad scientists now," Erin said as she pulled carelessly at wires in the robot's chest.

"There's nothing to it," Lawrence said, recklessly joining circuits inside one of the robot's brains.

"And Franny hardly did any of the work on this robot. It's really more our robot than hers," Phil added, and the robot beeped.

CHAPTER TWELVE

THE NEW ROBOT IS A SMASH HIT

Franny walked happily into her classroom. She was thinking about maybe rescuing more kids from stupid hobbies.

She was surprised, as anyone might be, to find that most of her classroom had been smashed to smithereens. (Note: For anybody doing the conversion, there are ten smithers in an ounce, and ten smithereens in a smither.)

Erin climbed from underneath a smoldering chunk of desk. "Thank goodness," she said. "Another mad scientist to help us."

Franny raised one eyebrow. "'Another' mad scientist? What do you mean by 'another'? *You're* not a mad scientist."

Lawrence and Phil climbed out from their hiding places. "Sure we are," Phil said. "You should have seen us yesterday."

"That's right," Lawrence added. "And we finished the robot last night."

"You finished it?" Franny shouted. "You're not qualified to do that. What made you think you could create and activate something that complex and dangerous?"

The three of them just looked down at their feet.

Then it suddenly occurred to Franny. *She* was what made them think that.

"I have a very bad feeling about this," Franny said.

CHAPTER THIRTEEN

FOOLS + TOOLS =
BUSTED-UP SCHOOLS

Franny scribbled some computations on the robot's blueprint. She reviewed the notes that Erin, Lawrence, and Phil had given her, and tried to include in her calculations what they could remember about the extra work they had done during the night.

They could hear the robot starting on a new rampage somewhere else in the school.

Franny finished her computations. "Egad," she gasped.

"What? What is it?" Lawrence squeaked.

"I designed the robot with two heads because, as you know, two heads would make it twice as smart as a regular robot."

Phil tried to look like he understood.

"But you guys, well, you don't know the first thing about robots, or electronics, or science, or machines, or maybe anything."

Erin scowled a bit, but this was no time to argue.

"You see, because you know nothing, you actually made this robot twice as *stupid* as a regular robot."

"So will that make it easier to stop?" Lawrence asked hopefully.

"Hand me my backpack," Franny said sternly.

CHAPTER FOURTEEN

STUPIDER AND STUPIDER

Franny took another dose of her invisibility formula. "It can't smash what it can't see," she said, trying her best to sound optimistic. And she faded from their sight.

Most monstrous fiends, even though they are often horribly destructive, have a plan. Either they want something, they hate something, or they're just trying to escape capture. So it's easy for a scientific mind to figure them out and stop them.

This thing is different, Franny thought. *This robot is pure stupidness. It has two whole heads full of stupid. Pure stupidness does things for no good reason.*

What would a pure-stupid creature do in a school? Franny thought.

Franny ran past a door on which the robot had left some graffiti. It was badly spelled, badly drawn, and not at all clever. "In addition," Franny said, "it's probably inaccurate. If the principal really *did* have a rubber butt, surely by now they would have flown her to consult with a medical expert in Switzerland."

Franny ran past gigantic spit wads that the robot had left dangling from the ceiling and dripping down the walls.

"Spit wads," she said. "Can you imagine wasting perfectly good spit this way? Spit, like most secretions, is hours of fun for a child with a microscope. Only an idiot would squander it this way."

Spitty robot footprints led right up to the library door, and Franny actually felt an unfamiliar wave of fear wash over her.

"Not the books," she said.

CHAPTER FIFTEEN

FRANNY KETCHES UP TO THE ROBOT

Franny slid quietly into the library. She knew the robot was in there somewhere.

She could have overlooked the graffiti. Franny had made inaccurate speculations about butts before. Butts are an imprecise science; errors occur.

And she might even have been able to find some merit in giant spit wads. She had to admit that they had a sort of charm to them, like a fresh snowfall—a fresh snowfall that smelled like the inside of somebody's mouth.

But Franny *loved* books. She loved everything about them. Most of what Franny knew she had learned from books. A creature this stupid could be in the library for only one reason: to destroy books. And an act that stupid was not going to be tolerated.

She moved silently and cautiously.

And then she heard it: the sad, sick sound of a page slowly being torn from a book. She crept through the aisles.

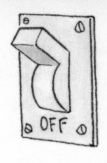

She rounded a corner and saw the robot there, happily destroying books. It was clear to Franny that this mechanical imbecile would not stop until it had destroyed all of them.

As she studied the horrible creation, she suddenly felt confident that defeating this robot was going to be quite easy. In fact, she felt very confident.

Evidently Erin, Lawrence, and Phil had installed an off switch right in the middle of the robot's chest.

All Franny had to do was quietly walk up to it, totally unseen, and flip the switch.

"Actually, that was pretty clever of them," Franny whispered, "to install an off switch in such a convenient location."

And if Franny had thought it through for just a split second longer, she would have realized that Erin, Phil, and Lawrence were not qualified to come up with something as clever as a chest-mounted off switch that would actually work.

But she hadn't thought it through, and she did *flip* the switch, which was not wired to turn off the robot, of course, but *was* wired to squirt a huge gush of ketchup from its newly installed ketchup nozzle.

The books! Franny leapt through the air and dove in front of a shelf full of books, hero-ically protecting them from the sloppy condi-ment onslaught but at the same time taking the full impact of the ketchup herself, thus rendering herself totally visible to the robot.

CHAPTER SIXTEEN
HERE, LET ME GIVE YOU A HAND

Crash! The robot smashed Franny with its giant hand.

Erin, Lawrence, and Phil heard it and rushed into the library.

"We'll save you, Franny!" they shouted. They folded their arms just like they had seen Franny do. "It's mad science time," they said.

The robot swung at Franny again. She tried to dodge, but it caught her hard. *SMASH!*

"Uh, got some mad science coming right up," the kids said, looking at each other helplessly. The robot's hand came down with another mighty crash. *BASH!* Franny didn't think she could last much longer.

Then Franny did what she did best. She *thought*, and she thought fast.

"Maybe, maybe a mad scientist is exactly what we *don't* need," she said. *SMASH!* She took another powerful slam from the robot's hand.

She looked over at her friends, and then it
suddenly came to her. Franny knew exactly
what they needed.

"What we need is a philatelist!" she yelled.

"A what?" Erin shouted back.

"A philatelist is a stamp collector," Phil said.
"Like me."

"Phil!" Franny yelled. "The eyes!"

Phil knew exactly what Franny meant. A pair of stamps would cover the robot's little square eyes perfectly. Phil pulled out a pair of stamps from his pocket and with a lick and a slap, had them across the robot's eyes.

Now blinded, the robot missed Franny entirely. And its metal hands were too big and clumsy to remove the stamps.

"Now what we need is an accordionist!" Franny shouted, and Lawrence leapt into action. Grabbing one of the robot's heads in his right hand and the other head in his left, Lawrence began flexing his powerful deltoid and trapezius muscles, built up by years of music lessons.

The robot reeled and fell under Lawrence's mighty accordionist blows.

"Now what we need is ...," Franny began, but Erin was already one step ahead of her.

"An Irish dancer," Erin said, and began hammering out a merciless hail of rhythmic stomps on the fallen robot, sending gears and wires in all directions.

When the dust finally settled, the four of them stood there looking at the pile of broken, flattened, robot parts.

It was over. They had won. They had been saved by philately, accordionism, and Gaelic choreography.

CHAPTER SEVENTEEN

NOW YOU'RE COOKING

Later, back at the lab, Franny and Igor were completing Franny's newest project. She had explained what had happened that day, and Igor wondered if Franny knew just how extremely lucky she was to have friends that were not mad scientists.

Franny put down her welding torch. "At last, it's complete," she said.

"Igor," Franny said, handing him a piece of paper, "run downstairs and get these items. Quickly; I'll need them for this next experiment."

Igor began to read the list as he ran: *Sugar, flour, milk...*

Franny picked up the phone and paused to look at her newest creation.

She dialed the phone. "Billy?" she said.

Igor walked in with the ingredients, bowls, and cookie sheets Franny had requested.

"How would you like to come up to the lab and, um, share some of your techniques with me?" Igor heard Franny say.

Erin's dance had stamped the robot into nice, flat pieces that Franny had spent a long time cutting and welding into what was probably the best pastry oven in the world.

Franny K. Stein, mad scientist, was going to bake pretty, pretty cookies.

"He'll be right over," Franny beamed, and Igor smiled.

Franny K. Stein
MAD SCIENTIST

THE FRAN THAT TIME FORGOT

Franny K. Stein
MAD SCIENTIST

THE FRAN THAT TIME FORGOT

JIM BENTON

For
Griffin, Summer, Mary K,
Dan, Barb, Bruce, Mom, and Dad

CONTENTS

Franny K. Stein
MAD SCIENTIST

THE FRAN THAT TIME FORGOT

CHAPTER ONE
FRANNY'S HOUSE

The Stein family lived in the pretty pink house with lovely purple shutters down at the end of Daffodil Street. Everything about the house was bright and cheery. Everything, that is, except the upstairs bedroom with the tiny round window.

That tiny round window looked in on the bedroom and laboratory of Franny K. Stein, Little Girl Mad Scientist.

Recently, in this very lab, Franny had created Zero Gravity Dog Food, to make walking her dog, Igor, more fun.

And before that, she had invented Cannibalistic Broccoli that ate itself, so kids who hated eating vegetables would never have to.

And she still had a giant, hamster-powered trike, which she had created when she was only three years old.

She had been a mad scientist since she was just a baby. And Franny had been building and accumulating her creations in this lab as long as she could remember.

And she was very, very serious about it. She always had been.

CHAPTER TWO
FRANNY'S FAMILY

The rest of Franny's family was not really interested in mad science.

Franny's dad was a regular dad. He loved Franny, but he didn't really appreciate her Voice-Activated Cheese Cannon, which provided the user with an endless supply of cheeseballs on demand. It just wasn't the sort of thing that regular dads appreciated.

And Franny's mom was a regular mom. She loved Franny, but she didn't really appreciate things like the special chicken that Franny had bred with so many wishbones that you could wish for anything you wanted.

And Franny's little brother, Freddy, was a regular little brother. He loved Franny too (of course, he'd never admit it).

Freddy didn't appreciate her creations either. Especially when he found them under his bed at night.

But even though they didn't always appreciate her creations, they had learned to take them seriously. When they didn't, it made Franny pretty angry, and the only thing more dangerous than a mad scientist is an angry mad scientist.

CHAPTER THREE
FRANNY TAKES THE CAKE

The announcement of the yearly Science Fair at school always filled Franny with mixed emotions. On the one hand, Franny loved creating new inventions and sharing them with others.

57. CREATE TALKING EGG SALAD

58. TURN BROTHER INTO PILE OF DIAPERS

59. BUILD MACHINE THAT CAN TRAVEL THROUGH TAPIOCA

60. MAKE A BAT-POWERED HELICOPTER

61. GROW SECOND HEAD

62. INVENT DEVICE THAT CHANGES BLACK JELLY BEANS INTO RED ONES.

63. CREATE ODOR THAT MAKES SKUNKS SICK

64. ....

65. TURN OCEANS TO COLA

66. MAKE

68. MAKE EVERYTHING MORE SCARY

On the other hand, Franny already had a long list of projects in her lab that she was anxious to complete.

And on the other hand, it was always an extra challenge to create a project that the kids at school would appreciate. Wait a second, that was *three* hands.

60. MAKE A BAT-POWERED HELICOPTER

61. GROW SECOND HEAD

62. INVENT DEVICE THAT CHANGES BLACK JELLY BEANS INTO RED ONES

63 CREATE ODOR THAT MAKES SKUNKS

64 TURN OCEANS INTO COLA

68 MAKE EVERYTHING MORE SCARY

Well, this is Franny we're talking about.

Franny explained it to her mom. "I want to do a good Science Fair project, but I really don't like to take time away from the other lab projects."

Her mom smiled. "You can't have it both ways, Franny. You know what they say: You can't have your cake and eat it too."

A wide grin came across Franny's face. "You can't have your cake and eat it too? We'll see about that."

Franny walked quickly to her lab, with the blueprint of her next creation beginning to form inside her head as she went.

CHAPTER FOUR

IT WAS A PIECE OF CAKE

Franny began assembling the mechanism she had designed. "Can't have your cake and eat it too," she scoffed. "Where do they come up with these things?"

As she worked, Franny recalled when she conducted experiments based on other sayings she had heard her mom use.

AN APPLE A DAY KEEPS THE DOCTOR AWAY.

But it has to Be a REALLY BIG APPLE.

A BIRD IN THE HAND IS WORTH TWO IN THE BUSH.

BUT ARE YOU SURE YOU WANT A BIRD IN YOUR HAND?

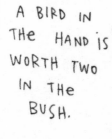

WHOEVER SAID "AS EASY AS TAKING CANDY FROM A BABY"

NEVER ACTUALLY TRIED TO DO IT.

At last her device was complete, and she demonstrated it to her faithful assistant, Igor.

"Observe. Here, on my Time Warp Dessert Plate, I have a delicious piece of cake." Igor nodded. He was always ready to observe a delicious piece of cake.

Franny gobbled it up quickly. "Now I've eaten it. So, of course, I no longer have it."

Igor shook his head. No cake. That IS sad.

"But through a slight time warp, I can actually make a small zone on the plate go back to a point in the recent past when I had not yet eaten the cake."

Igor's eyes widened as the cake reappeared on Franny's special plate.

"And now I have it again," she said.

There was a way to have your cake and eat
it too, and Franny had figured it out.

"Easy as pie," she said.

CHAPTER FIVE
FROM FAIR TO CLOUDY

Miss Shelly smiled as the principal of the school, Mrs. Pierce, addressed all of the students. "Thank you all so much for working so hard to make this year's Science Fair exciting and interesting and not, uh, life threatening," she said.

The other kids knew exactly what Mrs. Pierce was talking about. In years past, some of Franny's creations had been a bit dangerous.

REMOTE CONTROL SCISSORS

PORCUPINE UNDERPANTS

SUGAR FROSTED SNAKES

TORNADO IN A JAR

CHICKEN FINGERS

25

In fact, most of Franny's creations could be dangerous, and the kids had learned to be very, very careful around anything that came out of Franny's laboratory. They liked Franny, but they had learned to take Franny and her creations very seriously.

"We had many excellent entries, and this year we're giving out certificates," the principal said.

"I'm happy to present third prize to William Frederick Davis for his new breed of banana that you just turn inside out instead of peeling."

William smiled and ran up and took his certificate.

"I never knew his middle name was *Frederick,*" Franny whispered, and suddenly she looked a bit concerned.

"Second prize goes to Anthony Christopher Hernandez for his Never-Miss Baseball Glove." Anthony ran up and got his certificate.

"*Christopher*, huh?" Franny said, looking slightly more concerned.

"And first prize," the principal began, "again goes to Franny—"

"Uh, that's okay," Franny interrupted nervously. "I'll, uh, just pass on the certificate."

"Of course not," Mrs. Pierce said. "You won fair and square, Franny. You should be proud."

"Okay, but you don't have to read my name or anything. We all know my name."

"Nonsense," the principal said. "For her Time
Warp Dessert Plate, first prize goes to Franny
Kissypie Stein."

CHAPTER SIX

WHAT'S IN A NAME

Franny *Kissypie* Stein. The principal looked at the certificate more closely just to make sure she had read it correctly. She even cleaned her glasses.

"Is that right, Franny? Is your middle name 'Kissypie'?"

SCIENCE FAIR AWARD

Franny Kissypie Stein

TIME WARP DESSERT PLATE

1ST Prize

Franny walked up and quietly took the certificate.

"Yes," Franny said. "It is. My middle name is Kissypie."

The kids looked at the principal. They looked at Miss Shelly. They looked at Franny. They looked at each other.

And then they erupted into an explosion of laughter. Franny *Kissypie* Stein. They could hardly believe it.

"It's the most ridiculous name I ever heard!" one of the kids shouted.

"What kind of a middle name is that?"

"We've been afraid of a kid named Kissypie?"

Even Miss Shelly and the principal giggled a little. And Franny felt a terrible destructive rage start to boil inside her.

"Silence!" Franny yelled, and her eyes flashed with her terrible, mad scientist anger.

"You think I want Kissypie for a middle name? It was some stupid nickname my dad had for my mom when they were just dating. They thought it would be cute to give it to me. I never asked to be named Kissypie."

Franny's face reddened and she spoke through clenched teeth. "Just in case none of you know how it works, your *parents* name you. You don't name yourself. Don't you think I'd change it if I had a way?"

"I bet you would," one of the kids yelled, and they all started laughing even harder.

Franny was so angry that she started to tremble. She couldn't stand being laughed at. She was just about to do something truly awful when her eyes fell on her Time Warp Dessert Plate.

Franny whispered to herself. "Don't you think I'd change it if I had a way?" Her mind began the calculations. "I wonder..."

CHAPTER SEVEN

IT'S ONLY A MATTER OF TIME

Franny's mom watched as Franny carried calendars, watches, and hourglasses into her room. "More junk, Franny?" she said.

"I need this stuff, Mom. It's critical that I thoroughly understand the nature of time if this experiment is going to succeed."

"I know your experiments are important, Franny. But look at this room: bones everywhere, drawers full of guts. I suppose that banana peel is going to stay on the floor forever. Honestly, Franny, this is the sort of thing that attracts mice."

"I promise to clean it up, okay, Mom? But right now I have to finish this."

43

Franny's mom threw her arms into the air
and walked out, leaving Franny and Igor to the
experiment at hand.

CHAPTER EIGHT
I WONDER WHAT YESTERDAY WILL BE LIKE

I t's really not much more complicated than the dessert plate, Igor. It just needs to work on me, instead of the cake, and I just have to travel *farther* into the past."

Franny showed Igor a copy of her birth certificate. "Here's what I need to change. See where it says 'Kissypie'? I'm going back in time and changing it to something more dignified—something people won't laugh at."

She strapped her Time Warper Device to her arm. "Wish me luck," Franny said, and she pressed a button. There was a flash, a pop, and a little puff of smoke, and she was gone.

Igor was scared. He had no idea where Franny was or, more *frighteningly*, *when* she was.

CHAPTER NINE
DOWN MEMORY LANE

Franny hurtled back through time. She saw the time she faced a two-headed robot, a giant Cupid, and a Pumpkin-Crab Monster.

She saw the day she got Igor, the day she met Miss Shelly, and the day she first brought one of her teddy bears to life.

"I'm getting close," Franny said, and got ready to press the STOP button on the Time Warper.

She saw a familiar-looking baby girl in a bassinet in a hospital nursery.

"This is it," Franny said, and she pressed the button.

CHAPTER TEN

MAKING A NAME FOR YOURSELF

There was a flash, and a pop, and a little puff of smoke, and Franny stood there, directly in front of Baby Franny.

Baby Franny blinked in astonishment as Franny grabbed Baby Franny's chart.

"I'm doing you a huge favor," she said to Baby Franny. "I'm changing this dumb middle name so that nobody can ever make fun of it again."

Franny erased "Kissypie." "Let's see," she said. "I still want to keep the initial *K*. How about 'Kidney'? Do you like the sound of that?"

Baby Franny scrunched up her nose.

"No, huh?" Franny said. "Maybe 'Khufu,' or 'Kismet,' or 'Kilowatt'?

Baby Franny pulled the pacifier from her mouth. "Kaboom," she said.

Franny smiled. "It's a bit peculiar, but I like it. It's like an explosion," she said, and she wrote "Kaboom" down as her middle name. Then she leaned way down and said, very seriously, to Baby Franny, "The most important thing is that nobody will laugh at us again. *There is nothing worse than being laughed at.*"

She picked up Baby Franny's toy elephant. "Here, let me fix that for you," she said, and drew a few extra eyes on it.

With a flash, and a pop, and a little puff of smoke, Franny was gone.

Baby Franny looked at the elephant with the extra eyes and smiled. At that moment she knew she wanted to create more things like that doll. At that moment, Baby Franny became a mad scientist.

CHAPTER ELEVEN

THERE'S NO TIME LIKE THE PRESENT

Franny started hurtling forward again in time, back to the present. "I was kind of cute when I was a baby," she said, smiling.

"I wonder how I'll look when I'm older," she said, tapping her finger on her chin. (Franny was a very curious girl.)

"Since I have the Time Warper Device running, I guess it wouldn't hurt to have a little peek into the future," she said, and she went right past the present and into the future.

With a flash, and a pop, and a little puff of smoke, Franny found herself in front of her house, sometime in the future.

CHAPTER TWELVE
YOU SHOULD BE ASHAMED OF YOURSELF

At least, Franny thought this was her house. Thick smoke poured out of a huge chimney that punched out through the roof. Rusty drums of chemicals lay all over the yard. Terrible howls and screeches came from unseen creatures hiding within.

"I like what they've done with the place," Franny said approvingly. "I'm just surprised that Mom decided to go with this look. She's usually so fussy."

Franny eased her way past the front door, which was hanging by a single hinge. Inside, the living room was crawling with snakes and spiders and things that looked like maybe they were half snake and half spider. "Perhaps a bit much," Franny said. "Still, it's quite cozy."

There was no sign of her family anywhere.
Even Igor, who would have run to the door to
meet her, was gone.

She tiptoed up the stairs toward her bed-room laboratory and quietly pushed the door open.

STAY OUT

There, feverishly banging on a fiendish-looking device, was a tall mad scientist that Franny knew could only be herself as a teenager.

CHAPTER THIRTEEN

WILL YOU JUST LISTEN TO YOURSELF?

Teen Franny twisted the final screw on the machine she was constructing. "The Monster Multiplier is finally complete. They were foolish to laugh at me," she grumbled as she began throwing switches. The Monster Multiplier started to whine and sizzle.

"But no more. Let's see how they like it when these monsters begin overrunning the planet. Soon they'll take over the entire world. There'll be no laughing then."

The Monster Multiplier crackled. The door opened and out walked a monster. It looked a lot like the elephant toy she had decorated for Baby Franny, but a lot bigger.

It crackled again, and again the door opened. An identical elephant-monster walked out.

Soon the machine was making monster after monster. They jumped out the window and began waging terror on the streets. "It won't be long now," Teen Franny said, and she grinned a mad scientist smile—an evil mad scientist smile. "It won't be long before all the laughing stops."

Franny gasped. Teen Franny was pretty handy in the monster-making machine department, and you had to give her credit for that. But she was evil. She was way beyond an acceptable amount of evil. She was really and truly evil—the kind of evil that had to be stopped.

"I did this to myself," Franny said. "I never should have gone back in time, and I never should have changed my middle name."

And she never should have walked backward into the arms of a five-eyed elephant-monster, but she did that, too.

CHAPTER FOURTEEN

YOU SHOULD HAVE GOTTEN A GRIP ON YOURSELF BEFORE YOURSELF GOT A GRIP ON YOU

Teen Franny looked angrily at Franny, who was struggling to free herself from the arms of the five-eyed monster. "So what was it?" Teen Franny said. "Some sort of a time machine? Sounds like something I might do."

"That's exactly what I did," Franny said. "It's a beautiful, classic piece of mad science."

Teen Franny huffed and pushed one of her monsters out the window.

"Please," Franny said. "You have to stop this. I mean—don't get me wrong—I'm a huge fan of monsters, and I'm even fond of an occasional rampage. But what you're planning is beyond that. This is not just mad science. This is evil mad science. Why are you doing this?"

Teen Franny's eyes narrowed. "C'mon, Franny. You're me. You know why."

Franny shook her head. "Really, I don't."

Teen Franny cruelly flicked a spider with her finger. "The Science Fair, Franny. Remember the Science Fair?"

CHAPTER FIFTEEN

IS THERE AN ECHO IN HERE? IS THERE AN ECHO IN HERE?

I'll bet this is because I made my middle name too extreme," Franny whispered. "The name Kaboom is like an explosion. *This* version of me grew up with a name that sounded like utter destruction."

73

Teen Franny rummaged through a trunk.
"Here it is," she said, and she showed it to
Franny. Behind some cracked glass was the
certificate from the Science Fair made out to
Franny Kaboom Stein.

Teen Franny turned up her Monster Multiplier, and the monsters started popping out faster and faster.

"You asked me why I'm doing this, kid. It was because they laughed. They laughed at my middle name, and they laughed at me."

Franny thought, *Wait a second. They laughed at the name "Kissypie," but I had no idea that they would laugh at the name "Kaboom." They would have laughed at "Kismet" or "Khufu" or "Kidney." This had nothing to do with the name.*

Teen Franny spoke through clenched teeth. "The most important thing is that nobody will laugh at us again. *There is nothing worse than being laughed at.*"

Those were Franny's precise words coming back to haunt her. That was exactly what she had told herself as a baby.

Suddenly Franny understood that none of this was about changing her name to Kaboom. This was all because of what she had said to Baby Franny about laughing.

Teen Franny looked out the window as her monsters began tearing the neighbors' homes to pieces, and she smiled an evil smile.

Franny said to herself, "Think! Think! Think!"

CHAPTER SIXTEEN

ONE MORE REASON TO NEVER CLEAN YOUR ROOM

Franny couldn't get away, and she couldn't reach the controls on her Time Warper Device.

Suddenly a thought occurred to her.

Franny looked around and spotted her old Voice-Activated Cheese Cannon. "Cheddar!" she shouted, and caught the cannonball of cheese it launched her way.

Teen Franny spun around. "Hold it right there, kid," she said. "I know what you're thinking. You're thinking that cheese will attract the mice, and then the mice will scare the elephant-monster, which will drop you, and then you'll escape. Am I right?"

Franny said nothing.

"Of course I'm right," Teen Franny sneered. "I'm just as clever as you are, Franny. But two principles in your dumb little plan are entirely incorrect: Mice don't *really* like cheese, and elephants aren't *really* afraid of mice."

"I guess you're right," Franny said. "But *my* plan was based on the principle that nobody likes it when you stuff wads of cheese up their nose," she said as she did exactly that. "And I never, ever, ever cleaned up my room."

The elephant-monster, struggling to dislodge the cheese wad from its trunk, took two steps backward and slipped on the banana peel that had been in that exact spot for years, just as Franny's mom had predicted. As the monster fell, it released Franny.

85

Teen Franny lunged for one of the countless inventions lying around the lab. She aimed the Frog-O-Matic and fired it at Franny. Franny swiftly grabbed a mirror and deflected the ray.

Teen Franny picked up the electric Molecule Destroyer and switched it on. Franny quickly unplugged it from the wall.

"This is my lab too, you know," Franny said.
"I made most of this junk. I know how it
works," and she fired a Freeze Ray at Teen
Franny.

Teen Franny fired a Heat Ray back and the
rays cancelled each other out.

"Yeah," Teen Franny said. "I know how it all works too. And while we stand here battling, my elephant-monsters continue to multiply. And besides, you bratty little kid, we may be the same person, but I'm the older version. That means I know everything you know, plus a little bit more. You can't defeat me."

Franny knew that Teen Franny was right. She closed her eyes and thought as hard as she could.

Suddenly an idea came to her.

"Oh, yes I can," Franny said, and she pushed a button on the Time Warper Device. With a flash, and a pop, and a little puff of smoke, she was gone.

CHAPTER SEVENTEEN
HE WHO LAUGHS FIRST, LAUGHS LAST

F ranny was suddenly back at the Science Fair. Anthony Christopher Hernandez had just gotten his certificate for his Never-Miss Baseball Glove, and Franny looked very concerned, again.

"And first prize," the principal began, "again goes to Franny—"

"Uh, that's okay," Franny interrupted nervously. "I'll, uh, just pass on the certificate."

"Of course not," Mrs. Pierce said. "You won fair and square, Franny. You should be proud."

"Okay, but you don't have to read my name or anything. We all know my name."

"Nonsense," the principal said. "For her Time Warp Dessert Plate, first prize goes to Franny *Kaboom* Stein."

The principal looked at the certificate more closely just to make sure she had read it correctly. She even cleaned her glasses.

"Is that right, Franny? Is your middle name 'Kaboom'?"

Franny walked up and quietly took the certificate.

"Yes," Franny said. "It is. My middle name is Kaboom."

The kids looked at the principal. They
looked at Miss Shelly. They looked at Franny.
They looked at each other.

And then they erupted into an explosion of
laughter. Franny *Kaboom* Stein. They could
hardly believe it.

"It's the most ridiculous name I ever heard!" one of the kids shouted.

"What kind of a middle name is that?"

Even Miss Shelly and the principal giggled a little. And Franny felt a terrible destructive rage start to boil inside her.

Franny knew she had one chance to beat Teen Franny and the horrible future that awaited her if she did not.

I didn't have to change my name, she thought. *I had to change how I felt about people laughing at it.*

And Franny smiled.

And then she chuckled. And she laughed. "Kaboom," she said. "You're right, it is a pretty ridiculous name." And Franny suddenly didn't really mind the kids laughing. It was a silly name, and it made her laugh too.

There are a lot of things worse than being laughed at, she thought.

CHAPTER EIGHTEEN
A FUTURE WITH APPEAL

The next day Franny cleaned up the lab just like she had promised her mom. They cleaned up the drawers full of guts, organized the boxes of bones, and took Franny's first-place certificate out of the trunk and hung it proudly on the wall.

Franny even allowed herself another giggle at the name Kaboom. Laughing at yourself was much easier than she used to believe.

Franny's lab was still pretty cluttered, but it looked better than ever, and Franny knew, deep down, that she would never, ever, ever grow up into the evil Teen Franny she had seen on her journey into the future.

Of course, they left the banana peel right where she might need it to be . . .

just in case.